THE TROLL MUSIC

Story and Pictures
by
ANITA LOBEL

HARPER & ROW, PUBLISHERS • NEW YORK

Typographic design by Natalie Shalita

for my husband

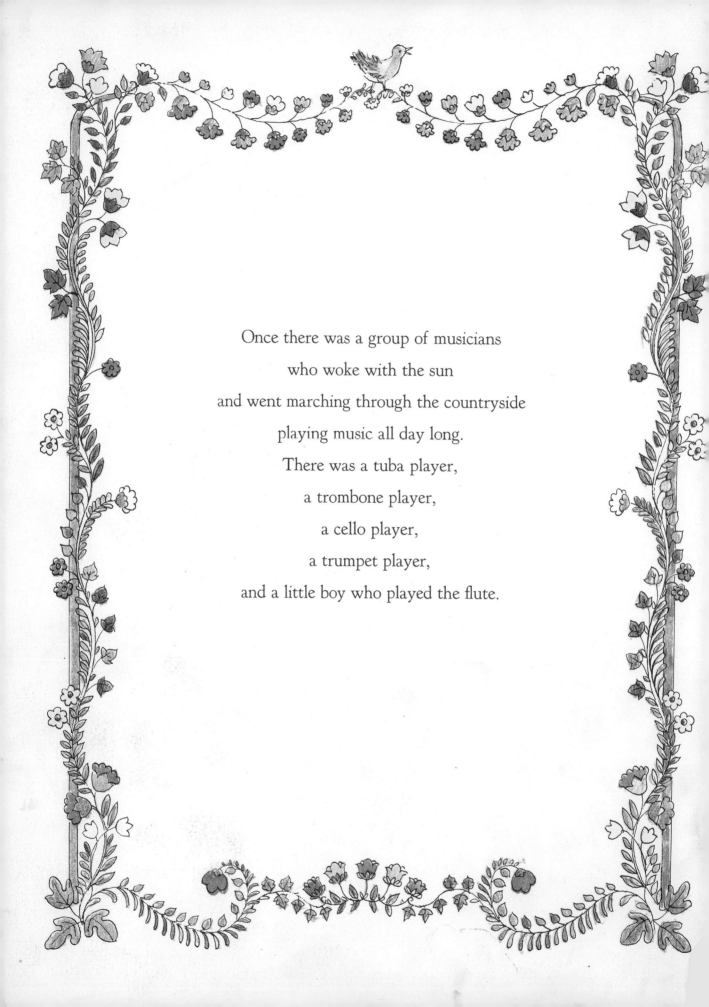

Once there was a group of musicians
who woke with the sun
and went marching through the countryside
playing music all day long.
There was a tuba player,
a trombone player,
a cello player,
a trumpet player,
and a little boy who played the flute.

They played in villages and towns.
They played for kings and shoemakers,
for ladies and for children.
And wherever they went, everyone agreed
that their music was the best in the land.

One evening,

after a long day of playing music,

the musicians fell asleep at the edge of a forest

under a large tree.

A troll came by and saw the sleeping musicians

and their shiny instruments.

"Ah, music, music in the moonlight," he thought.

"I could sing and dance, if I heard some music!"

He poked the musicians with a stick,

then he kicked them with his foot.

He climbed a tree and shook acorns down on them.

But the tired players slept soundly on and on.

The troll became angry.

"Wake up! Wake up!" he screamed. "I want some music!"

The little flute player woke up and was surprised

to see an angry troll.

He picked up his flute to play a soothing tune.

But the troll was so angry

at the other sleeping musicians

that he just growled,

"Small boys should be asleep at this time of night!"

He swished his tail over the musicians,

grumbled some magic words, and disappeared.

In the morning the musicians woke up,

picked up their instruments,

and went to the next town.

Many people were in the square,

waiting for the music to begin.

"Moo-o-o," went the tuba.

"Baa-a-a," went the cello.

"Neigh, neigh," went the trombone.

"Honk, honk," went the trumpet.

"Cluck, cluck, cluck," went the flute.

The people who had come to listen

to the most beautiful music in the land

became very angry and threw sticks and stones

at the musicians, who fled as fast as they could.

Outside of the town gates they began to cry.

"What has happened to our beautiful music?" they sobbed.

The musicians tried to play their instruments again.

"Moo‑o‑o," went the tuba.

A cow thought she heard another cow

and wandered over the field to look.

"Baa‑a‑a," went the cello,

and a lamb came looking for a friend.

"Neigh, neigh," went the trombone,

and a horse galloped toward them over the meadow.

"Honk, honk," went the trumpet,

and a goose came to listen to the goose she heard.

"Cluck, cluck, cluck," went the flute,

and a little hen came and joined the other animals.

From a nearby tree a nasty laugh was heard.

A creature with a tail grinned at them

through the leaves.

"That's the troll who did it!"

cried the flute player. "He did it!

He put a magic spell on our music

last night when you were asleep."

"Quick, let's play something for him!" said the musicians,

grabbing their instruments.

But only the friendly animals liked their music now,

and the troll just chuckled and disappeared.

"What shall we do? What shall we do?"

moaned the musicians.

"People will never listen

to our music and clap for us again.

Oh, what shall we do?"

"Moo-o-o," the cow said with sympathy.

"Honk, honk," said the goose sadly.

And the horse galloped around, neighing

in a pleasant way.

"Baa-a-a," said the lamb to the cello player.

And the hen said, "Cluck, cluck, cluck,"

and laid an egg.

"I think I know what to do," the flute player cried.

"These animals can help us make some nice things.

We will take them to the troll

and try to exchange them for our music."

The others were puzzled at first,

but as they watched the flute player dance around,

holding up the egg the little hen had laid,

they began to understand.

The hen laid many eggs.

The lamb gave some wool.

The cow gave milk, and the goose shed feathers.

The horse ran to a nearby town

and brought many things they would need.

The musicians baked a cake.

From the lamb's wool they wove some cloth

and knit a sweater.

From the cloth and the goose feathers they made a pillow.

The flute player made a wreath of flowers.

Then they put everything on the horse's back

and went to look for the troll.

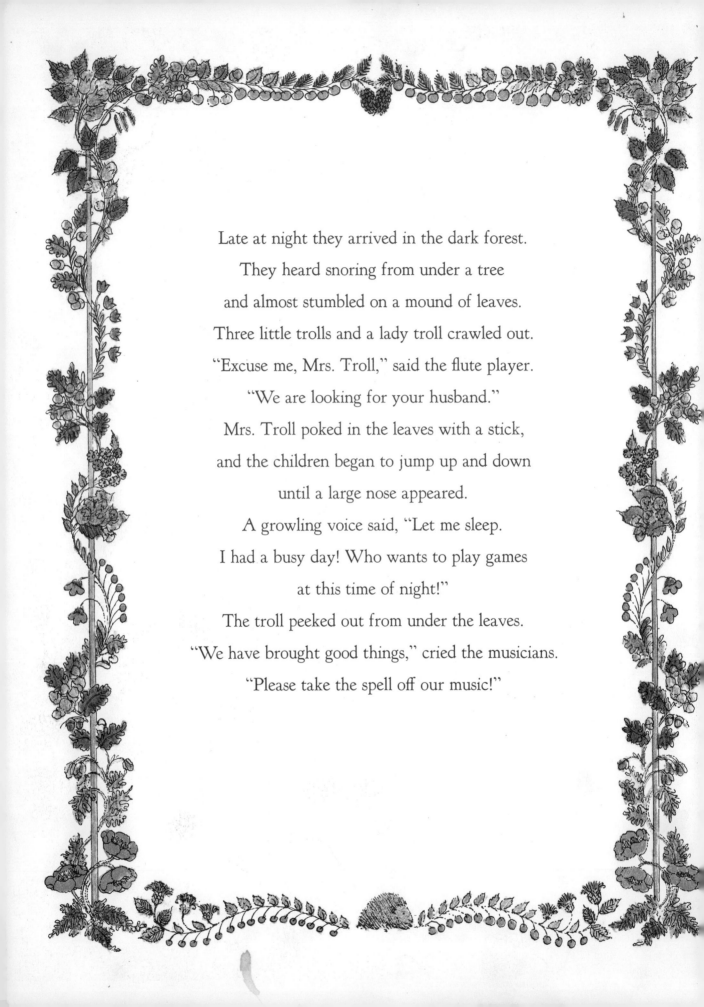

Late at night they arrived in the dark forest.

They heard snoring from under a tree

and almost stumbled on a mound of leaves.

Three little trolls and a lady troll crawled out.

"Excuse me, Mrs. Troll," said the flute player.

"We are looking for your husband."

Mrs. Troll poked in the leaves with a stick,

and the children began to jump up and down

until a large nose appeared.

A growling voice said, "Let me sleep.

I had a busy day! Who wants to play games

at this time of night!"

The troll peeked out from under the leaves.

"We have brought good things," cried the musicians.

"Please take the spell off our music!"

"Spell? Have you been
running around mumbling magic words again?
For shame!" said Mrs. Troll.
And she punched her husband in the nose.
He ran to hide in a tree.
Mrs. Troll looked happily at all the presents.
She sat on the pillow
and put the flower wreath on her head.
She tasted the cake.
The troll children ate some cake
and went for a ride on the horse.
"I want some cake," cried the troll from his tree.
Mrs. Troll went on eating.
After a while she said very sweetly,
"This might be a real party if we had some music."
"We would play for you," said the flute player,
"but we can't."

"I want some cake,"
said the troll.
"Take the spell off
and you may have some,"
said Mrs. Troll.

"Don't hit my nose again," said the troll.
"No more spells," said Mrs. Troll. "Promise?"
Climbing out of the tree, the troll looked
at the cake and grinned at the musicians,
but he did not promise a thing.
He did mumble strange magic words
and swish his tail three times at the moon.

"Now play!" he said to the musicians,
and he went to eat his cake.

The musicians tried their instruments,

not knowing what to expect.

But the tuba did not moo.

The cello did not baa.

The trombone did not neigh.

The trumpet did not honk.

The flute did not cluck.

And the music sounded better than ever.

When the animals heard the beautiful new sounds

the instruments made, they began to dance,

and everyone else joined in.

And they all sang and ate cake and played games.

It was a splendid party.

In the morning the musicians woke up,
said good-bye to the trolls, and thanked the animals.
They picked up their instruments, started playing, and marched
out of the forest.
When they arrived at the next town, the people clapped
and cheered.
"The musicians are back," someone cried.
"And listen! Their music sounds more beautiful than ever!"

And everyone agreed that it was true.